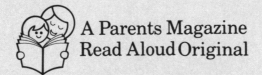

Get Well, Clown-Arounds!

by
Joanna Cole
pictures by
Jerry Smath

Parents Magazine Press
New York

Library of Congress Cataloging in Publication Data
Cole, Joanna. Get well, Clown-Arounds!
Summary: A wacky family thinks that they have
become sick when they look in the mirror and see
green spots.
[1. Sick—Fiction.   2. Humorous stories]
I. Smath, Jerry, ill.   II. Title
PZ7.C67346Ge   1983   [E]   82-8148
ISBN 0-8193-1095-6   AACR2
ISBN 0-8193-1096-4 (lib. bdg.)

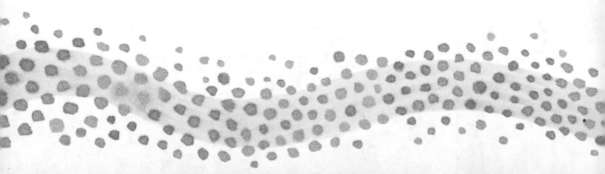

To Julian Azcarate—J.C.

To Margaret and Ed Harnish—J.S.

It was a busy day at the Clown-Arounds'
house. Mrs. Clown-Around was washing
the windows.

Mr. Clown-Around was fixing the car.

And Bubbles and Wag-Around were
planting a garden.

Baby was busy too. She was trying out
her new paint set.

She painted pink stripes on the floor.

She painted red squiggles on the wall.

And she painted green spots
on the mirror.

Mr. Clown-Around scolded Baby
and washed off the red squiggles.

Mrs. Clown-Around scolded Baby and
washed off the pink stripes.

But no one noticed the green spots
on the mirror.

Then Mr. Clown-Around went
to comb his hair.
He looked in the mirror.
"Uh-oh," he thought.
"I must be very sick!"

So Mr. Clown-Around went right to bed.

Bubbles looked in the mirror while she brushed her teeth.

And Mrs. Clown-Around held Baby up while she looked at her new hat.

"Help!" cried Mrs. Clown-Around. "We must be very sick!"

Now the whole Clown-Around family was in bed.

Mrs. Clown-Around called Dr. Bozo.

Dr. Bozo examined the Clown-Arounds carefully. But he could not find anything wrong.

Dr. Bozo walked up and down,
thinking very hard.

He walked past the mirror.

Oh no! Now Dr. Bozo was in bed too!

The Clown-Arounds were
in an awful pickle.
Everyone was in bed—even the doctor!
There was only one thing to do.

Bubbles quickly wrote a note
and gave it to Wag-Around to deliver.

Wag-Around followed his nose
and found the right house.

GRANDMA
CLOWN-
AROUND

He delivered the note
to Grandma Clown-Around.

It said:

Dear Grandma,
We are all sick.
Please come
and help.

Love,
Bubbles

Grandma Clown-Around hurried right over.
First, she made a big pot of her
famous chicken soup.

While the soup was cooking, Grandma
mopped the floor and
dusted the furniture.

She even polished the mirror.

Then she fluffed up the pillows
and gave everyone some hot chicken soup.

In no time, Mr. Clown-Around felt better.
He got up and looked in the mirror.

Mrs. Clown-Around was next.

Then Baby, Bubbles, and Dr. Bozo.

How wonderful—
there were no green spots anywhere!

Everyone gave Grandma Clown-Around
a big thank-you hug.

Because the Clown-Arounds think that
Grandma's chicken soup is
the best medicine ever.
Don't you?

About the Author

JOANNA COLE, author of the Clown-Around stories, finds herself thinking about these characters often. After the first two stories were written, she began comparing everything her family did with what the Clown-Arounds do. "And when we all came down with the flu," Ms. Cole says, "I couldn't help but wonder how the Clown-Arounds would get along if they got sick." And that's how *Get Well, Clown-Arounds!* was born.

Ms. Cole was an elementary school teacher and a children's book editor before turning to writing full time. She now writes books for and about children.

Ms. Cole, her husband, and daughter, live in New York City.

About the Artist

JERRY SMATH does free-lance illustration
for magazines and children's school
books. He wrote and illustrated two
books for Parents, *But No Elephants* and
The Housekeeper's Dog. He also drew
the pictures for both *The Clown-Arounds*
and *The Clown-Arounds Have a Party* by
Joanna Cole. "It's been a lot of fun
making Joanna's Clown-Arounds come to
life," says Mr. Smath. "I hope I've done
justice to Joanna's lively imagination."

Mr. Smath and his wife, Valerie, a
graphic designer, live in Westchester
County, New York.